The Midnight Circus

The Midnight Circus

PETER COLLINGTON

ALFRED A. KNOPF · NEW YORK

This is a Borzoi Book published by Alfred A. Knopf, Inc.

Copyright © 1992 by Peter Collington

All rights reserved under International and Pan-American Copyright Conventions. Published in the United States by Alfred A. Knopf, Inc., New York. Distributed by Random House, Inc., New York. Originally published in Great Britain in 1992 by Heinemann Young Books. Manufactured in Italy   1 2 3 4 5 6 7 8 9 10

Library of Congress Cataloging-in-Publication Data
Collington, Peter. The midnight circus / by Peter Collington.   p.   cm. Summary: A young boy's favorite mechanical horse comes to life and carries him to a circus for a night of adventure and stardom.
ISBN: 0–679–83262–9 (trade)   ISBN: 0–679–93262–3 (lib. bdg.)
[1. Circus—Fiction. 2. Horses—Fiction. 3. Toys—Fiction. 4. Stories without words.]
I. Title   PZ7.C686Mi   1992   [E]—dc20   91–39535

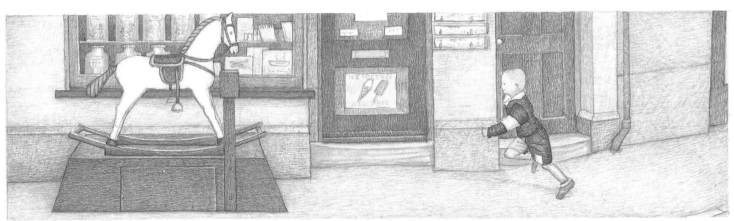

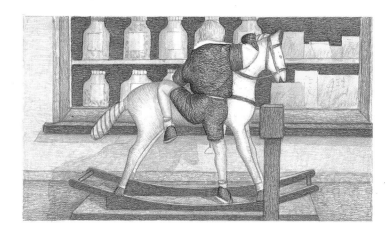

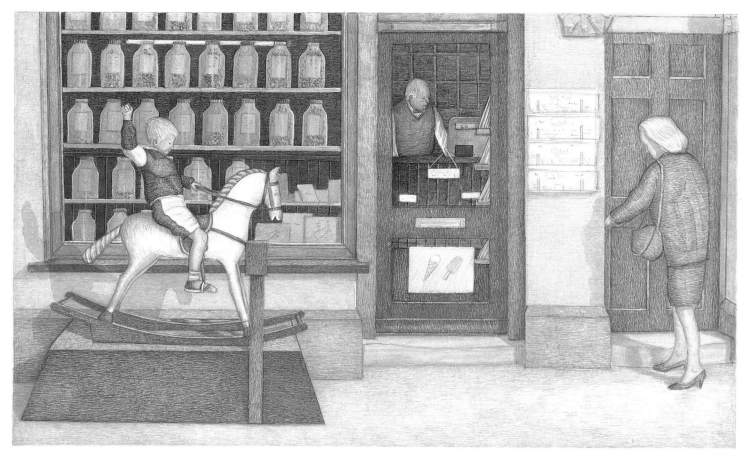

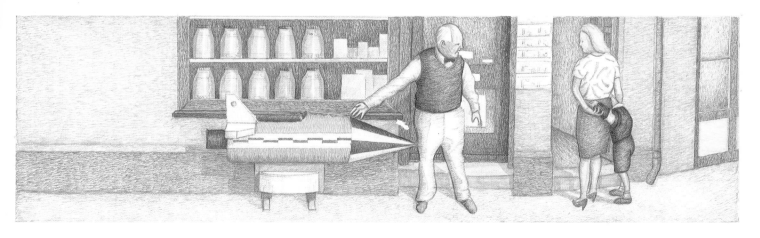

THE CIRCUS FAMILY

Book-Mark

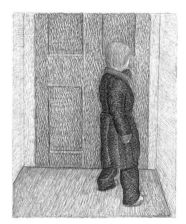

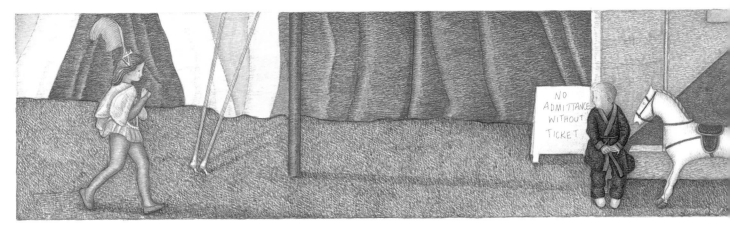

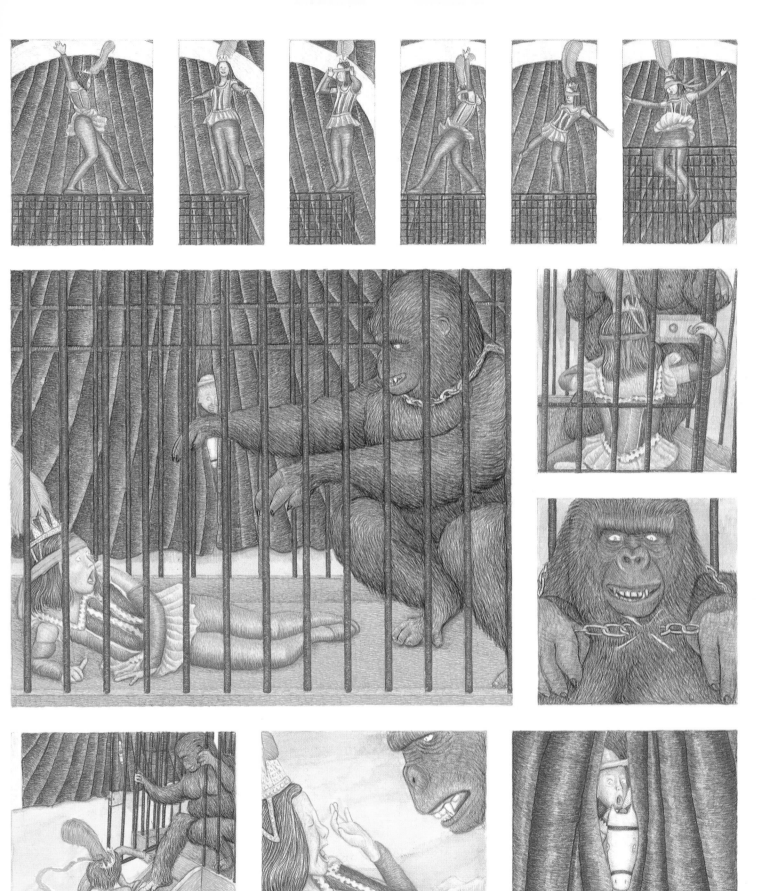

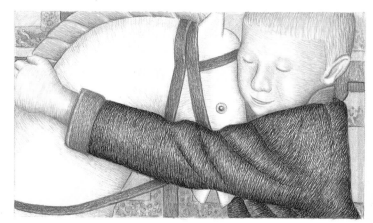

LL
P
COL

Collington, Peter

The Midnight Circus

05/07	**DATE DUE**		